WEIRD FACTS TO BLOW YOUR MIND

Illustrated by Skip Morrow

Written by Judith Freeman Clark & Stephen Long

A New England Publishing Associates Book

PRICE STERN SLOAN
Los Angeles

D0057481

Illustrations copyright ©1993 by Skip Morrow
Text copyright ©1993 by Judith Freeman Clark, Stephen Long,
and New England Publishing Associates, Inc.

Cover Design: Don Brunelle and Skip Morrow

A New England Publishing Associates Book

Published by Price Stern Sloan, Inc.
11150 Olympic Boulevard, Los Angeles, California 90064

ISBN: 0-8431-3579-4

Library of Congress Catalog Number: 93-12251

Library of Congress Cataloging-in-Publication Data

Clark, Judith Freeman.
    Weird Facts to blow your mind by Judith Freeman Clark;
illustrated by Skip Morrow.
        p. cm. — (Facts to blow your mind)
    Summary: A collection of interesting trivia and informative facts.
    ISBN 0-8431-3579-4 : $4.99
    1. Curiosities and wonders — Juvenile literature. (1. Curiosities
and wonders.) I. Morrow, Skip, Ill. II. Title. III. Series:
Clark, Judith Freemen, Facts to blow your mind.
AG243.C5639   1993
031.02 — dc20   93-12251
                                                      CIP
                                                      AC

Table of Contents

LORD CORNBURY

MOTHER NATURE'S LITTLE JOKES

Feeling Blue?

Doctors had heard of families in Kentucky called the "blue people," but nobody knew much about them until 1962. Then, scientists began a study that finally showed these "blue bloods" have a rare condition with the almost unpronounceable name of methemoglobinemia. This cuts down the production of the red blood cells, which carry oxygen through the body and give blood its red color. Your skin turns blue when you don't have enough red blood cells. Only a handful of people have this strange disorder. Most of them belong to the same, large family. You'll recognize them if you ever meet them. Their skin is the color of blue jeans!

Darlings! You Look Good Enough To Eat!

When people fall in love, they usually treat each other nicely. It's a little different with some other members of the animal kingdom. Certain insects have strange, even deadly, mating rituals. The black widow spider is probably the most famous. This lovely arachnid can be charming during courtship—but she gets her name from her deadly behavior. Once she finishes mating, she eats her partner. She also is fickle. A single black widow spider may mate with and consume up to 25 males in a single day!

Earthshaking News

Scientists may not be able to predict earthquakes, but cows and worms can. Often before an earthquake here's what can happen. Cows become restless and stand still, with their legs far apart. The water in wells goes up or down. Worms crawl out of the ground, and snakes slither from their dens. So, if the ground is suddenly alive with creepy, crawly creatures, if the well overflows, or if the cows won't budge— better run for it!

Not Gone And Not Forgotten

Imagine what the headlines would be if scientists discovered a living dinosaur. "Impossible," you say, "the dinosaurs that roamed Earth millions of years ago are all now extinct." Are you so sure? Scientists were once absolutely convinced other species were long since extinct. Working their nets in waters off the coast of Africa one day in 1938 fishermen caught an unusual fish. It was 5 feet long and weighed over a hundred pounds, with ugly, gray-blue scales and strong, snapping jaws. Scientists investigated and said it looked exactly like fossilized remains of Coelacanths. This fish lived in the time of dinosaurs, millions of years ago, but no one believed they still existed. Soon, several more Coelacanths were found living deep in the pitch-black waters off the African coast. Who knows what else might be down there?

All Ears

Bats are pretty ugly, but add a pair of oversize ears as big as wings, and you've got one strange creature. The Townsend's Big-eared Bat has a body that is only about 4.5 inches long, including its tail. But attached to its tiny head are ears nearly 3 inches long that droop halfway to the tip of its tail.

Christmas In July?

Almost everyone looks forward to summer, when the weather's warm enough to go swimming, walk around barefoot and have picnics. Imagine how surprised and cheated everyone must have felt in 1816, the year without a summer. It was all due to a volcanic eruption in what is now Indonesia. Thick, black ash from the explosion formed a cloud that hid the sun for months. All over the eastern United States and much of the Northern Hemisphere there was nothing but dense cloud cover. Temperatures fell to below freezing at night. New England was hit by a blizzard that dropped nearly a foot of snow in June! As far south as Georgia, the temperature on July 4th was only 46 degrees Fahrenheit.

Toad-ally Weird

In many parts of the world, farmers keep cats in their barns to chase rodents away from oats and other grain used for feeding livestock. In some parts of South America, however, farmers use giant, 5-pound Marine toads to protect stored grain from mice and rats. These toads don't even have teeth. What they do have are huge mouths filled with poison spit. One gulp and a rodent is trapped and fatally paralyzed inside the toad's deadly maw.

Pop Goes The Cockroach!

One way to get rid of cockroaches without using poison is to spread boric acid on the floor. When the roach eats the boric acid, it gets terrible gas. Unfortunately for it, a roach can't burp to let the gas out. As a result, its stomach just expands until it pops.

I Wish I Were Big!

Many kids, especially boys, hope to grow up tall. Sometimes kids get impatient with their height—it's too hard for them to wait until they reach their full growth in their late teens. Some years back, a young Austrian man named Adam Rainer must have felt very worried about his size. Although he was 21 years old, he wasn't even 4 feet tall! It's easy to guess that he disliked the word dwarf, which is the word doctors used to describe him. It's also easy to imagine that he wished he were taller. Perhaps the young man wished too hard. He suddenly started growing one day. Soon, he was over 7 feet tall! He was nearly 8 feet tall when he died in 1950, the only person known to have been a dwarf and a giant in a single lifetime!

Almost Enough For Twins

Mothers and fathers usually get very excited over the birth of a baby. They joke about who the baby looks like and play little games with its toes and fingers. In 1921 two English parents must have been surprised when playing "This Little Piggy" with their new baby. They discovered that the baby had 14 fingers and 15 toes—a record.

Barnyard Recycling

Recycling of household items is sweeping the country now, but farmers and cows have been doing it for decades. Cows love to eat grass and hay but often swallow things they can't chew easily, like bits of metal. Because of this, farmers sometimes give each cow a magnet to swallow. Since a cow has four separate stomachs, the magnet does not pass through the cow's digestive system. Instead, it stays in one stomach, where it attracts nails, pieces of wire and other metal the cow swallows while grazing. When the cow is butchered, the magnet is taken out of its stomach. The farmer then sells the metal stuck to the magnet to a recycling company!

Ready, Aim, Fire!

Most wild animals need a good defensive strategy to keep from ending up as another animal's dinner. But few creatures have weapons as effective as the porcupine's: each is covered with 30,000 sharply barbed quills. When riled, the porcupine swats his enemy with his tail, and the enemy ends up with a face looking like a pin cushion!

Shocking, Isn't It?

Every year, lightning strikes thousands of people and kills about 150 Americans. A lightning bolt, which can be 20 miles high, can carry 100 million volts of electricity and is five times hotter than the sun's surface. You'd think lightning victims would be burned to a crisp—but they're not. People electrocuted by lightning show absolutely no markings on their bodies!

Instead Of Brushing, Get A Bird

After devouring another animal, a crocodile usually feels like taking a nap. It crawls onto a riverbank, stretches out in the sun, and drifts off to sleep with its mouth wide open. Small birds—plovers—take care of its teeth. The plovers dash in and out of the croc's open mouth, picking morsels of leftover meat from between the reptile's sharp, pointed teeth. This way, the croc avoids dental problems and the plovers get a free lunch.

What Goes Around Comes Around

Minks, weasel-like creatures, suffer from a severe form of dizziness called Meniere's Syndrome. A mink troubled by this disorder whirls around in circles, chasing his tail. When he catches it, he bites the tip of his tail and grabs on, hoping to steady himself. Instead, he can end up chewing down the entire length of his 10-inch tail in a crazy effort to end his dizzy spell.

My, How You've Grown

Parents sometimes say their kids have "shot up overnight" because the kids have grown taller very quickly. Scientists who have measured kids daily have found that such statements may be literally true. Kids would stay one height for days, then one day they would suddenly be taller. One boy they measured grew more than a half-inch overnight!

Bug Spray

When a grasshopper gets angry, it has a sure-fire way of ridding itself of unwanted attention: it aims a stream of smelly, brown liquid at its enemies. The grasshopper produces this gunk in a special gland in its body. About the worst it can do to you is stain your skin or clothes, but smaller creatures—like spiders or other insects—can become sick or even paralyzed after being sprayed with "grasshopper juice."

Termites And Lions Beware!

Of all the world's animals, the aardvark is among the most peculiar. Sometimes called the earth pig or the antbear, this native of Africa likes to burrow in the ground, probing with its 12-inch-long tongue for its favorite foods: ants and termites. It's a bad idea to annoy these anteaters. Aardvarks are so fierce—and well-equipped with sharp claws—that they sometimes attack and kill lions.

Open Wide!

A fish known as the Black Swallower can devour other fish two to three times bigger than itself. That's because its mouth, throat, and stomach can stretch like balloons—and its teeth can lie down flat in its mouth. Even so, sometimes one of these porkers bites off more than he can chew, and both fish die.

A Royal Stinger

Queen honeybees take royalty seriously. They won't even sting a common worker bee, only another queen. While a worker bee usually loses its stinger and dies after stinging, a queen keeps her stinger in place and can use it over and over again. The instinct to stab another queen is so strong that she will repeatedly sting a rival queen even long after her victim is dead.

Asleep On Your Feet?

Horses sometimes go for months without lying down, but they don't lose any sleep because of that. In fact, they sleep an average of 8 to 10 hours a day. Horses sleep better on their feet than on their sides because their lungs don't work well when they lie down. A horse's leg muscles are controlled by reflex actions in the spine, rather than in the brain. This enables a horse to catch itself, should it start to fall over, without ever waking up.

Eager Beaver

Scientists have discovered that the main reason beavers build dams is that they can't stand the sound of running water. By building a dam, the beavers make a still pond out of what was once a gurgling stream. Beavers hate the sound of water so much they have been tricked into trying to dam up a loudspeaker playing the sound of running water.

THE ULTIMATE IN FOOD & DRINK

Pass The Castor Oil!

Some mental illnesses make people do strange things. In the case of a sick Canadian woman, this odd behavior meant eating all sorts of unusual objects. Doctors learned of her problem when she complained of a terrible stomachache. Nothing could be done to stop her pain, so doctors performed emergency surgery. When they opened her stomach, the doctors found that the woman had swallowed more than 2,500 strange things. Nearly half of them were bent pins.

Wear Old Shoes When You Drink Beer

If you see someone drunk, don't let them shine their shoes. They could get sick and possibly die! Scientists discovered that a person drinking beer can be poisoned by breathing the fumes of nitrobenzene in shoe polish. When vapors from this chemical mix with the alcohol in a person's bloodstream, the combination is lethal! Medical records show that a man who had his shoes shined went out for a beer, then died a few hours later. The cause was finally determined to be nitrobenzene poisoning.

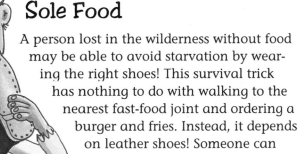

Sole Food

A person lost in the wilderness without food may be able to avoid starvation by wearing the right shoes! This survival trick has nothing to do with walking to the nearest fast-food joint and ordering a burger and fries. Instead, it depends on leather shoes! Someone can actually stay alive by chewing on leather shoes because the leather contains some basic nutrients that keep humans healthy.

The Worms Crawl In, the Worms Crawl Out

On some islands in the South Pacific, a popular food is the sea-worm. These creatures are gathered up from the ocean and baked in leaves along with crab meat—although people also like to eat them raw!

Here's The Beef!

Japanese beef is probably the most highly prized meat there is. In fact, Japanese cattle are so well cared for that even humans should be envious! To make sure its meat will be extra tender, a Japanese steer is given beer to drink every day and eats rice and beans instead of hay or grass. The fortunate animal also has a daily bath, and is massaged by hand three times a day with special Japanese gin!

Unfortunately, all this pampering can't save the steer from ending up on a dinner plate!

A Cool Idea

In some parts of Siberia the temperature dips way below freezing for most of the winter. That's why in Siberia milk is sold on a stick— frozen solid— rather than in a carton or bottle. You thaw it when you want to pour yourself a glass!

Eat-It-All

One of the strangest news stories of the 1960s featured a Frenchman, Monsieur Mangetout, who said he could eat glass and metal. Reporters who interviewed him found his claims were true. Over a time, the man devoured 10 bicycles, seven TV sets, and a small airplane!

The man, whose name means "Mister Eat-it-All," was checked by doctors, who at first did not believe what the reporters told them. But the doctors found he did, indeed, have a unique ability to digest as much as 2 pounds of metal every day!

Potatoes a La Mud

The Quechua Indians of Peru eat lots of potatoes. Because the spuds sometimes aren't quite ripe when they're dug up, Quechua cooks have found a way to improve the taste: they spread mud all over them. To the Quechuas, mud makes the potatoes a lot yummier—sort of like ketchup on french fries.

Japanese Roulette

One of the world's weirdest food customs involves deliberately flirting with death. In Japan it is a long-standing custom to eat raw fish, or sushi. One type, a blowfish called fugu, is a particular favorite. However, several hundred people die each year from eating fugu because parts of it are extremely poisonous! Only licensed chefs are allowed to prepare fugu because they're trained to remove the poisonous portions of the fish. Despite this danger, the Japanese look forward to fugu season—between October and March—so they can tempt their taste buds and risk their lives to eat raw fish!

Please Pass The Spider Plant

Kids eat the darndest things! Each year in the United States, poison control centers receive more than 75,000 calls about kids who have eaten house plants, unusual objects, and things they find outside. Some kids have a condition known as pica, which gives them uncontrollable cravings for paint chips, dirt, coal, clay and plaster!

Forget The Sleeping Pills

If you ever have trouble sleeping, maybe you should tuck into a turkey dinner. Turkey is full of a chemical called tryptophan, which is an important amino acid. It's also a natural sleep-inducer. Other foods that contain tryptophan are bananas and milk.

I Have A Tickle In My Throat

One popular student fad in the 1960s involved doing something most people would only try once, because it literally made their stomachs churn. Students competed to see who could swallow the most live goldfish. The record holder ate nearly 200, one right after another, each of them wiggling frantically as he gulped them down!

I Scream, You Scream

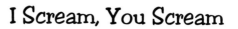

Next time you ask for a double-dip cone or a hot fudge sundae remember this: an important ingredient in ice cream is a stabilizer. This helps the flavorings, sugar and cream stay mixed together and prevents chunks of ice from forming in the ice cream. But you might want to forget what the most widely used ice cream stabilizer is: seaweed!

Stone Soup

In Japan, the bonito is a popular fish delicacy. A favorite way of preparing it is to boil it, smoke it, allow it to mildew, and then dry it in the sun until it is rock-hard. Treated this way, the bonito remains edible for about 10 years and is served in soup or stew.

ATTENTION GETTING BEHAVIOR

Getting A Buzz

Some people will do almost anything to get a little attention! A Pennsylvania man once came up with a great publicity stunt to get himself in the Guinness Book of World Records. He allowed himself to be covered with bees—live bees, about 100,000 of them. The man let the bees sit anywhere and everywhere on his body, except around his mouth. Altogether, the bees weighed some 28 pounds when they covered him—but the man was not stung even once!

I Wouldn't Do That If You Paid Me!

Kids dare each other to do all sorts of things—to ride a bike down a steep hill, or to jump over a stream without getting their feet wet. Some adults also will do strange or risky things when challenged—like the Chicago man who once ate a 2-inch cockroach on a dare. He won $200 from his friends for downing the insect!

I Remember You

Lots of people like to kiss, but affection can be shown in many ways. Some Polynesians put their hands in a friend's armpits, then rub their hands over their bodies so the friend's scent will stay with them all day.

Waiter, Bring Me A Pillow

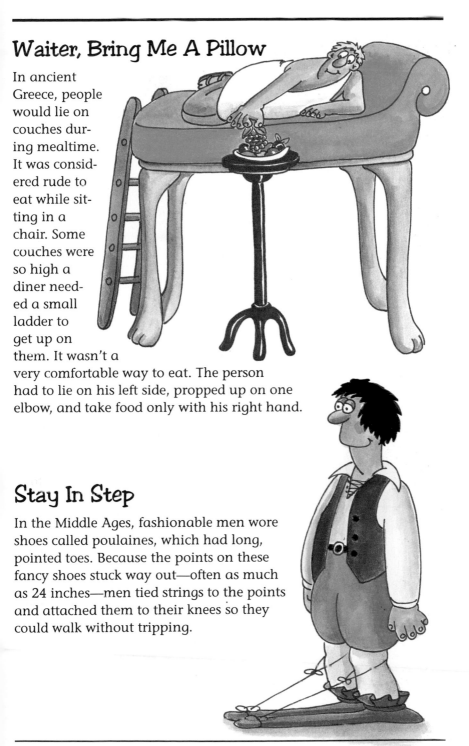

In ancient Greece, people would lie on couches during mealtime. It was considered rude to eat while sitting in a chair. Some couches were so high a diner needed a small ladder to get up on them. It wasn't a very comfortable way to eat. The person had to lie on his left side, propped up on one elbow, and take food only with his right hand.

Stay In Step

In the Middle Ages, fashionable men wore shoes called poulaines, which had long, pointed toes. Because the points on these fancy shoes stuck way out—often as much as 24 inches—men tied strings to the points and attached them to their knees so they could walk without tripping.

Please Pass The Soap

The bathtub has been around in some form or other since ancient times, and early bath tubs usually were round. People stood up in them, rather than sit down as we do. In England, by the Middle Ages, tubs had grown larger and longer, not to make them more comfortable but more efficient and economical. Bigger bath tubs saved on soap and water by permitting a large group of naked, dirty people to bathe together.

I Was Only Dreaming

When your foot goes to "sleep," how do you get rid of that "pins and needles" feeling? An early American remedy suggested that you spit on your finger, mark a cross on your foot, and in that moment your foot will recover.

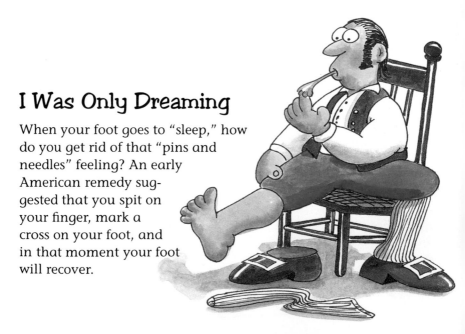

Woolly-minded?

In some marshy areas of France, shepherds used to stand on tall stilts to guard their sheep. The men also carried a long pole to lean or sit on. While thus poised above the bog, watching over their woolly charges, the shepherds whiled away the hours by knitting.

Did She Use That Greasy Kid Stuff?

Hairdo fashions have changed a lot over the years. When your parents were teenagers, many girls wore "beehive" hairstyles and boys had short haircuts known as "flat-tops." Two hundred years ago, when George Washington was president of the United States, men and women put on white, powdered wigs for dress-up occasions. One of the strangest hair fashions in human history was practiced in ancient Egypt. Before a dinner party or banquet, an Egyptian woman put a cone-shaped lump of sweet-smelling grease on top of her head. For many hours afterward, the cone would melt, slowly dripping through her hair and scenting it with perfume!

On The Level

Hundreds of years ago, Native American tribes in the Pacific Northwest thought that flat foreheads were beautiful. If a baby's head was not flat enough, the parents would wrap its head tightly in bands of animal hide and leave the binding on until the child was nearly 2 years old.

You Look Absolutely Gorgeous!

In the early 1700s, the royal governor of New York and New Jersey, Lord Cornbury, was well known for his favorite pastime: dressing up in women's clothes. He even had his official portrait painted while wearing a lady's ball gown. Eventually, Lord Cornbury was fired from his job as governor—for accepting bribes.

LORD CORNBURY

Watch Your Step . . . It's Slippery In Here

What people think about manners and cleanliness changes with time and place.

Nowadays, in most countries, it's not considered quite polite to spit on a public street. It's even against the law in some places. In China, however, spitting in public is not totally taboo. In the United States, shortly after the American Revolution, it was quite acceptable for people to spit on the floors of their homes!

You Look Like An Animal

Because Arctic winters are so cold, Eskimos have found some very creative ways to stay warm. In the past, they kept their feet cozy by wearing slippers made from whole birds turned inside out. They made raincoats from seal guts, and they sewed polar bear fur to the soles of their boots so they could walk silently through snow while hunting.

Just Call Me Stretch

A Spaniard named Georgius Albes, who lived during the 1650s, was famous for a peculiar reason: he was able to stretch his skin farther than anyone else. Albes could pull the skin from his chest up over one ear and stretch the skin on his neck to fold completely over his chin!

May I Have This Dance?

If a rat bit you during the Middle Ages, you might get sick with the plague, or "Black Death," as it was often called. In your agony, you might have ended up performing St. Vitus' Dance—a horrible set of symptoms brought on by the disease. Sufferers often gathered in large crowds near a church to pray for a cure. They were in such pain, they completely lost control of themselves, jerking arms and legs in the air, screaming loudly, crying and foaming at the mouth like mad dogs.

WAR IS WEIRD

The Atlas Of Smells

In the 1700s, Joseph Priestly, an English inventor and scientist, came up with a gadget called the eudiometer, which could test whether oxygen in the air was tainted with gas. French General Napoleon Bonaparte was so impressed by this invention that he formed a eudiometry company in his army to test air quality before a battle and to draw up a "bad smells" map of Europe.

Bats In The Belfry

One of the strangest military plans in recent history involved the use of bats. During World War II, the U.S Army planned to arm bats with tiny bombs, then release the flying mammals over enemy territory! More than 2 million bats were rounded up in Texas. The animals were stored in caves while scientists puzzled over ways to attach 1-ounce bombs to the animals' bodies. Although the military invested several million dollars in the plan, the bats were never called to active duty.

Cheese And Crackers, Anyone?

History books tell a strange story of a battle between the South American countries of Argentina and Uruguay in the 1840s. When defending their country against an invasion by Argentina, people in Uruguay's capital of Montevideo ran out of cannonballs. If they couldn't find some substitute ammunition, they would lose the battle. Imagine their delight when they discovered a supply of very old Edam cheese, which is formed into balls when it is made. The clever people of Uruguay loaded the cannon with cheese, won the battle and saved their country!

Who Knows?

When his troops invaded Korea during the 1500s, a Japanese warlord needed proof of the death of the soldiers on the losing side. His solution? He ordered that the dead Koreans noses be hacked off and then brought to Japan for burial!

First, Take The Cap Off The Tube . . .

The U.S. military spends hundreds of billions of tax dollars each year, much of it on training. Among the foes soldiers and sailors must be prepared to defeat is tooth decay. According to one source, the U.S. Navy spent more than $30,000 on a short film on tooth-brushing techniques. In all, the military produced 12 different movies on the subject!

Foul Play!

Today, biological or germ weapons are against the rules of war. But during the Middle Ages—sometimes called the Age of Chivalry—germ warfare was common, even though no one knew what a germ was! Troops used giant sling-shots to hurl rotten bodies of dead animals over castle walls at their enemies. They even used the corpses of soldiers who died from disease in the hope that illness would spread among enemy troops and kill them!

The Heat Of Battle

The British Army's decision to switch from traditional wool uniforms to polyester outfits led to a military fiasco during the 1982 war with Argentina in the Falkland Islands. The first time the new uniforms were worn in combat, 400 soldiers were badly hurt—not by bullets or bombs, but by uniforms that melted whenever the soldiers got too close to a fire.

See You Much Later, Dear

In ancient Sparta, young men were required to join the army at age 20 and to live in the barracks, even if they were married. Occasionally, however, they were allowed to visit their wives. The soldiers stayed in the army until they were 30. That's when they became full citizens and returned home to live.

Don't Run Off, Ok?

In Peru, archaeologists have uncovered graves of ancient warriors who died in battle and had been buried with all their helmets, shields, and weapons—as well their wives, servants and dogs. The corpses and their belongings were well preserved, but the feet of some of the servants had been cut off before burial, maybe to be sure they did not leave the warrior alone.

Turn-Coats

During the American Revolution, General Johnny Burgoyne punished soldiers who behaved badly by making them wear their uniform jackets inside out. The records tell us General Burgoyne's regiment was one of the most well behaved in the entire army.

Jewelry For A Special Occasion

Native Americans of different tribes at one time saved some pretty gruesome stuff as battle trophies—scalps, for example. One Cheyenne medicine man proudly wore a necklace strung with beads and the dried fingers of his fallen enemies.

AGAINST THE ODDS

Truth Is Stranger Than Fiction

Have you ever known of a coincidence weird enough to frighten you? Anne Parrish, a novelist, did in the 1920s when she was traveling in Europe. In a used-book store in Paris, she picked up a worn copy of a book. It was a collection of fairy tales she remembered reading when she was growing up in Colorado. Upon opening the book, she saw these words written on the inside cover in her own handwriting: "Anne Parrish, 209 N. Weber Street, Colorado Springs."

I Like It Up Here!

The next time you're in a plane flying high in the sky, don't bother worrying about whether your plane will crash into another plane. Experts say the chances of midair collisions are tiny. The time to worry is when you're on the ground. About 90 percent of airplane collisions take place on the ground at airports. Looks like we're safer up there than down here.

What's Your Favorite Number?

Many superstitions surround the number 13. One is that when 13 people sit down together at dinner, the first to get up from the table will be the first to die. Just a silly superstition? Not for the wife of British painter William Powell Firth (1819-1909). The Firths gave a dinner party for 11 friends, so that 13 sat at the table. After dinner, Mrs. Firth stood up, joking she was the most dispensable of the group. Her friend Mrs. Brooks also rose and said, "I'll be the second, for if you died, I wouldn't want to live." In one month, Mrs. Firth was dead. Her dear friend Mrs. Brooks died four months later.

Look Into The Crystal Liver

The ancient Etruscans believed they could foretell the future by carefully studying livers. Before planning an event or making a decision, Etruscan priests would stare at a just-killed sheep's liver to get the gods' advice.

United In Death

The second and third U.S. Presidents—John Adams and Thomas Jefferson—were political opponents, as well as friends later in life. On July 4, 1826, the 50th anniversary of America's Declaration of Independence which the two men had co-authored, Adams died at sunset at his home in Massachusetts. His last words were "Thomas Jefferson still survives." Adams didn't know that his old friend had died a few hours earlier at his home, Monticello, in Virginia—hundreds of miles away.

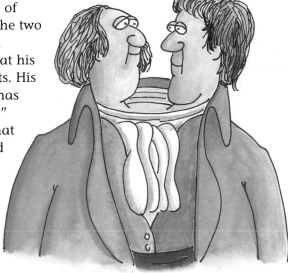

ALL SORTS OF WEIRDNESS

Dave's Not Here

When people are lost, they are afraid of nearly everything—even their rescuers. Sometimes, lost people will hide from those who are looking for them. After the first day of being lost, most frightened kids don't answer when they hear their names called, and by the second day, most adults won't answer either. Experts refer to this as the "bogey-man complex," an irrational fear that rescuers intend to hurt them.

If You Can't Beat 'em, Join 'em

There were no rabbits in Australia until 1850, when three pairs of English bunnies were set loose there. Ten years later they had become a national nuisance. Rabbits had no natural enemies in Australia, so they multiplied fast. Grass needed to raise cattle and sheep was nibbled down to the roots by millions of the long-eared creatures. Australians fought back by importing weasels, ferrets, and mongooses—all of which supposedly just love hunting rabbits. But instead of eliminating the bunnies, these new pests attacked the Australians' chickens. Finally, the Aussies solved the problem by raising rabbits and marketing rabbit meat and fur around the world.

Rest In Peace, Kitty.

Lots of people enjoy cats, but the ancient Egyptians carried cat-loving to extremes. They executed anyone who killed a cat! To show respect for a dead cat, its owner would shave his or her eyebrows off and even make a mummy of the deceased feline. More than 300,000 cat mummies have been discovered in Egyptian tombs!

Set Your Course On That Pig!

Hogs are such great swimmers that in the 1500s and 1600s explorers took them on voyages to help them discover new lands. Sailors thought hogs would instinctively swim toward the nearest land when thrown overboard. Unfortunately, the hogs often badly scratched their throats and necks with their sharp hoofs while thrashing through the water and bled to death before they could reach shore.

Stick It In Your Ear

Native Americans had several strange cures for earache. The Mohegans thought that inhaling tobacco smoke and blowing it into the ear of the sufferer would relieve the pain. Kickapoos boiled beans in water and then poured the liquid into the afflicted ear!

Practice! Practice! Practice!

Painters in India who made small portraits called miniatures used brushes with only one hair in them. They often spend 10 years learning to paint this way before they were allowed to complete a work of art on their own.

There's Gold In Them There Sheep!

Thousands of years ago, people in Turkey used sheepskins to filter gold dust out of the rushing waters of mountain streams. The gold would stick to the grease in the sheepskins, which were then dried out and put in a fire. When they burned up, clumps of melted gold were left behind.

Ding, Dong, ZAP!

In Medieval Europe, people thought that the sound of bells could break up thunderstorms. So whenever it rained, bell-ringers were sent to church steeples to pull the ropes that rang the chimes. The problem was that lightning often struck these tall steeples. The government of Paris finally prohibited bell-ringing during thunderstorms. During one 30-year period, more than 100 people were killed by lightning while hanging onto wet bell ropes!

A Real Barn-Burner

Farmers who store hay in their barns must be careful of a mysterious phenomenon known as spontaneous combustion. If the hay is damp when tossed into the barn, it can ferment and produce heat in the center of the hay pile. The hay can get so hot that it can burst into flames!

What Time Is It?

There are 24 time zones throughout the world, so somewhere it is morning once each hour. China covers five time zones but has decided that it should always be the same time in all parts of the nation. This means sunrise happens later and later as you travel west in China. In the city of Jixi the sun comes up at 5:00 a.m. But it's after 9:00 a.m. when the sun rises in the western city of Kashi!

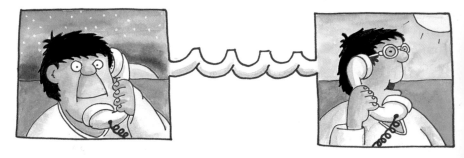

Water, Water, Everywhere

The world's oceans contain many freshwater springs. Usually, by the time the freshwater bubbles to the surface it's so mixed with saltwater that it's undrinkable. Islanders in the Persian Gulf and the South Pacific get around this problem by diving down to these freshwater springs and collecting drinking water in bags before it becomes too salty to drink.

Shocking, Isn't It?

In London during the 1700s, people suffering from all sorts of ailments went to the Temple of Health. One exhibit featured electricity, which had just been discovered, in a contraption called the "magnetico-electrico" bed. Couples who wanted to have children were told that lying on this bed would increase the wife's chances of becoming pregnant. Around the same time in Germany, another popular experiment involved putting young boys inside a machine so they could be the conductors of electricity when the machine was hooked up to an electrical source.

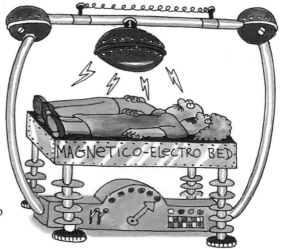

All-purpose Candles

Until the 17th century, candles often were made from tallow, or animal fat. Because of this, Roman soldiers often ate their candles rather than go hungry. The same was true of British lighthouse keepers, who often were cut off from food and other supplies during stormy weather.

Candles also were used to keep track of time. In coffee houses where auctions were often held, a pin was stuck into the side of a candle at the start of bidding. When the pin fell out, the auction was over. This custom gave birth to the expression, "to hear a pin drop."

Gimme A Shot Of Pig Juice

Insulin was discovered in the early 20th century. People with diabetes take insulin to help their bodies process and use sugar. This important substance is manufactured from the glands of sheep, pigs, oxen and other domesticated animals.

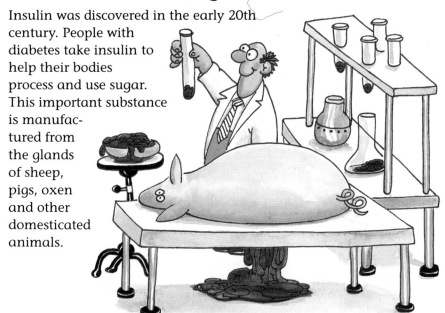

Weird Fact!!!

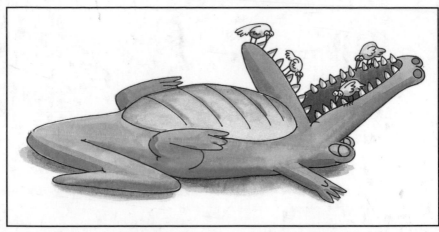

After devouring another animal, a crocodile usually feels like taking a nap. It crawls onto a riverbank, stretches out in the sun, and drifts off to sleep with its mouth wide open. Small birds—plovers—take care of its teeth. The plovers dash in and out of the croc's open mouth, picking morsels of left-over meat from between the reptile's sharp, pointed teeth. This way, the croc avoids dental problems and the plovers get a free lunch.

Within this book are more than 80 other truly **Weird Facts to Blow Your Mind** – not to mention the minds of your friends, teachers and, of course, parents!

Don't miss the other titles in this mind-blowing series:

Gross Facts to Blow Your Mind
Awesome Facts to Blow Your Mind
Scary Facts to Blow Your Mind

Cartoonist **Skip Morrow**'s previous books include *The Official I Hate Cats Book* and *The Second Official I Hate Cats Book*, both of which were bestsellers.

Judith Freeman Clark is a freelance writer. Her previous books include *The Almanac of American Women* and *The Gilded Age*.

Stephen Long is a produced playwright and tends a flock of black sheep at his home in Vermont.

ISBN 0-8431-3579-4

$4.9
$6.99 Canad

PRICE STERN SLOAN
Los Angeles